Yeh-Shen

A Cinderella Story from China

retold by Ai-Ling Louie
illustrated by Ed Young

PHILOMEL BOOKS
New York

To my Grandmother and my Mother

The story as it appears in *The Miscellaneous Record of Yu Yang*, a book which dates from the T'ang dynasty (618–907 A.D.). The author was one Tuan Ch'eng-Shih. Tuan's book was subsequently incorporated in an encyclopedic work which went through many editions. Shown here is the *Hsueh Chin T'ao Yun* edition from the Ch'ing dynasty (1644–1912). This modern reissue still uses the original block-printed page. The oldest European version of *Cinderella* was found to be an Italian tale from 1634.[1] Since the Yeh-Shen story predates that tale, Cinderella seems to have made her way to Europe from Asia.

[1]Iona and Peter Opie, *The Classic Fairy Tales* (London: Oxford University Press, 1974), p. 119.

Text copyright © 1982 by Ai-Ling Louie. Illustrations copyright © 1982 by Ed Young. Published by Philomel Books, a division of The Putnam & Grosset Group, 345 Hudson Street, New York, NY 10014. Published simultaneously in Canada. All rights reserved. Manufactured in China. Calligraphy by Jeanyee Wong. Typography by Nanette Stevenson.

Library of Congress Cataloging in Publication Data. Louie, Ai-Ling. Yeh-Shen. SUMMARY: A young Chinese girl overcomes the wickedness of her stepsister and stepmother to become the bride of a prince. [1. China—Fiction. 2. Stepchildren—Fiction. 3. Princess—Fiction] I. Young, Ed. II. Cinderella. III. Title. PZ7.L94Yc 1982 [Fic] 80-11745 ISBN 0-399-20900-X (hardcover) 20 PaperStar 0-698-11388-8

南人相傳秦漢前有洞主吳氏土人呼為吳洞娶兩妻
一妻卒有女名葉限少惠善陶鈞（一作金）父愛之末歲
父卒為後母所苦常令樵險汲深時嘗得一鱗二寸
餘頳鬐金目遂潛養於盆水日日長易數器大不能
受乃投於後池中女所得餘食輒沈以食之女至池
魚必露首枕岸他人至不復出其母知之每伺之魚
未嘗見也因詐女曰爾無勞乎吾為爾新其襦乃易
其弊衣後令汲於他泉計里數百（一作里）也母徐衣其
女衣袖利刃向池呼魚魚即出首因斫殺之魚已
長丈餘膳其肉味倍常魚藏其骨於鬱棲之下逾日
女至向池不復見魚矣乃哭於野忽有人被髮麁衣
自天而降慰女曰爾無哭爾母殺爾魚矣骨在糞下
爾歸可取魚骨藏於室所須第祈之當隨爾也用
其言金璣衣食隨欲而具及洞節母往令女守庭
女伺母行遠亦往衣翠紡上衣躡金履母所生女認
之謂母曰此甚似姊也母亦疑之女覺遽反遂遺一

隻履為洞人所得母歸但見女抱庭樹眠亦不之慮
其洞隣海島島中有國名陀汗兵強王數十島水界
數千里洞人遂貨其履於陀汗國國主得之命其左
右履之足小者履減一寸乃令一國婦人履之竟無
一稱者其輕如毛履石無聲陀汗王意其洞人以非
道得之遂禁錮而拷掠之竟不知所從來乃以是履
棄之於道旁即遍歷人家捕之若有女履者捕之以
告陀汗王怪之乃搜其室得葉限令履之而信葉限
因衣翠紡衣躡履而進色若天人也始具事於王載
魚骨與葉限俱還國其母及女即為飛石擊死洞人
哀之埋於石坑命曰懊女塚洞人以為禖祀求女必
應陀汗王至國以葉限為上婦一年王貪求於魚
骨寶玉無限逾年不復應王乃葬魚骨於海岸用珠
百斛藏之以金為際卒徵卒畔時將發以贍軍一夕
為海潮所淪成式舊家人李士元所說士元本邕州
洞中人多記得南中怪事

In the dim past, even before the Ch'in and the Han dynasties, there lived a cave chief of southern China by the name of Wu. As was the custom in those days, Chief Wu had taken two wives. Each wife in her turn had presented Wu with a baby daughter. But one of the wives sickened and died, and not too many days after that Chief Wu took to his bed and died too.

Yeh-Shen, the little orphan, grew to girlhood in her stepmother's home. She was a bright child and lovely too, with skin as smooth as ivory and dark pools for eyes. Her stepmother was jealous of all this beauty and goodness,

for her own daughter was not pretty at all. So in her displeasure, she gave poor Yeh-Shen the heaviest and most unpleasant chores.

The only friend that Yeh-Shen had to her name was a fish she had caught and raised. It was a beautiful fish with golden eyes, and every day it would come out of the water and rest its head on the bank of the pond, waiting for Yeh-Shen to feed it. Stepmother gave Yeh-Shen little enough

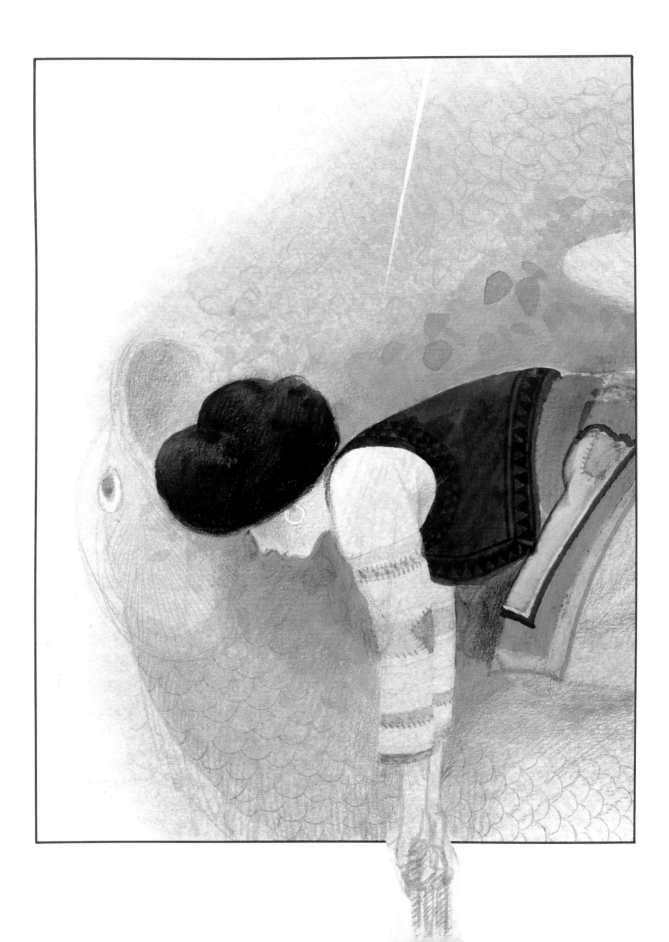

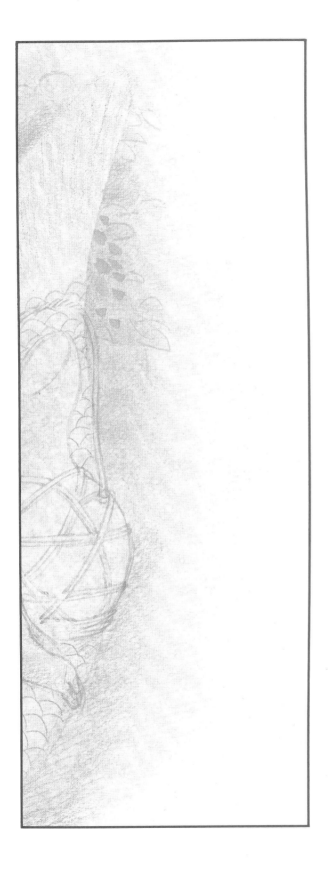

food for herself, but the orphan child always found something to share with her fish, which grew to enormous size.

Somehow the stepmother heard of this. She was terribly angry to discover that Yeh-Shen had kept a secret from her. She hurried down to the pond, but she was unable to see the fish, for Yeh-Shen's pet wisely hid itself. The stepmother, however, was a crafty woman, and she soon thought of a plan. She walked home and called out, "Yeh-Shen, go and collect some firewood. But wait! The neighbors might see you. Leave your filthy coat here!" The minute the girl was out of sight, her stepmother slipped on the coat herself and went down again to the pond. This time the big fish saw Yeh-Shen's familiar jacket and heaved itself onto the bank, expecting to be fed. But the stepmother, having hidden a dagger in her sleeve, stabbed the fish, wrapped it in her garments, and took it home to cook for dinner.

When Yeh-Shen came to the pond that evening, she found her pet had disappeared. Overcome with grief, the girl collapsed on the ground and dropped her tears into the still waters of the pond.

"Ah, poor child!" a voice said.

Yeh-Shen sat up to find a very old man looking down at her. He wore the coarsest of clothes, and his hair flowed down over his shoulders.

"Kind uncle, who may you be?" Yeh-Shen asked.

"That is not important, my child. All you must know is that I have been sent to tell you of the wondrous powers of your fish."

"My fish, but sir . . ." The girl's eyes filled with tears, and she could not go on.

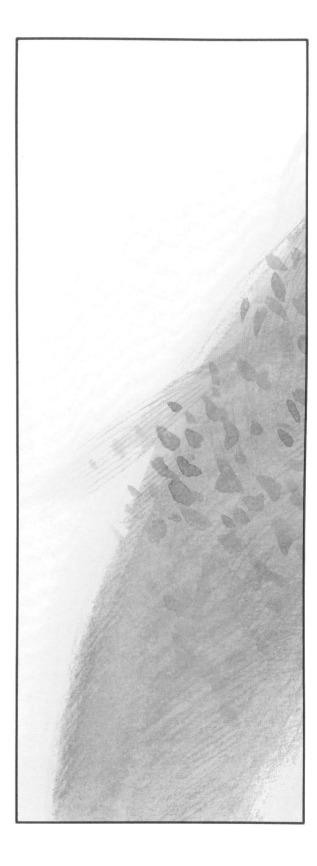

The old man sighed and said, "Yes, my child, your fish is no longer alive, and I must tell you that your step-mother is once more the cause of your sorrow." Yeh-Shen gasped in horror, but the old man went on. "Let us not dwell on things that are past," he said, "for I have come bringing you a gift. Now you must listen carefully to this: The bones of your fish are filled with a powerful spirit. Whenever you are in serious need, you must kneel before them and let them know your heart's desire. But do not waste their gifts."

Yeh-Shen wanted to ask the old sage many more questions, but he rose to the sky before she could utter another word. With heavy heart, Yeh-Shen made her way to the dung heap to gather the remains of her friend.

Time went by, and Yeh-Shen, who was often left alone, took comfort in speaking to the bones of her fish.

When she was hungry, which happened quite often, Yeh-Shen asked the bones for food. In this way, Yeh-Shen managed to live from day to day, but she lived in dread that her stepmother would discover her secret and take even that away from her.

So the time passed and spring came. Festival time was approaching: It was the busiest time of the year. Such cooking and cleaning and sewing there was to be done! Yeh-Shen had hardly a moment's rest. At the spring festival young men and young women from the village hoped to meet and to choose whom they would marry. How Yeh-Shen longed to go! But her stepmother had other plans. She hoped to find a husband for her own daughter and did not want any man to see the beauteous Yeh-Shen first.

When finally the holiday arrived, the stepmother and her daughter dressed themselves in their finery and filled their baskets with sweetmeats. "You must remain at home now, and watch to see that no one steals fruit from our trees," her stepmother told Yeh-Shen, and then she departed for the banquet with her own daughter.

As soon as she was alone, Yeh-Shen went to speak to the bones of her fish. "Oh, dear friend," she said, kneeling before the precious bones, "I long to go to the festival, but I cannot show myself in these rags. Is there somewhere I could borrow clothes fit to wear to the feast?" At once she found herself dressed in a gown of azure

blue, with a cloak of kingfisher feathers draped around her shoulders. Best of all, on her tiny feet were the most beautiful slippers she had ever seen. They were woven of golden threads, in a pattern like the scales of a fish, and the glistening soles were made of solid gold. There was magic in the shoes, for they should have been quite heavy, yet when Yeh-Shen walked, her feet felt as light as air.

"Be sure you do not lose your golden shoes," said the spirit of the bones. Yeh-Shen promised to be careful. Delighted with her transformation, she bid a fond farewell to the bones of her fish as she slipped off to join in the merrymaking.

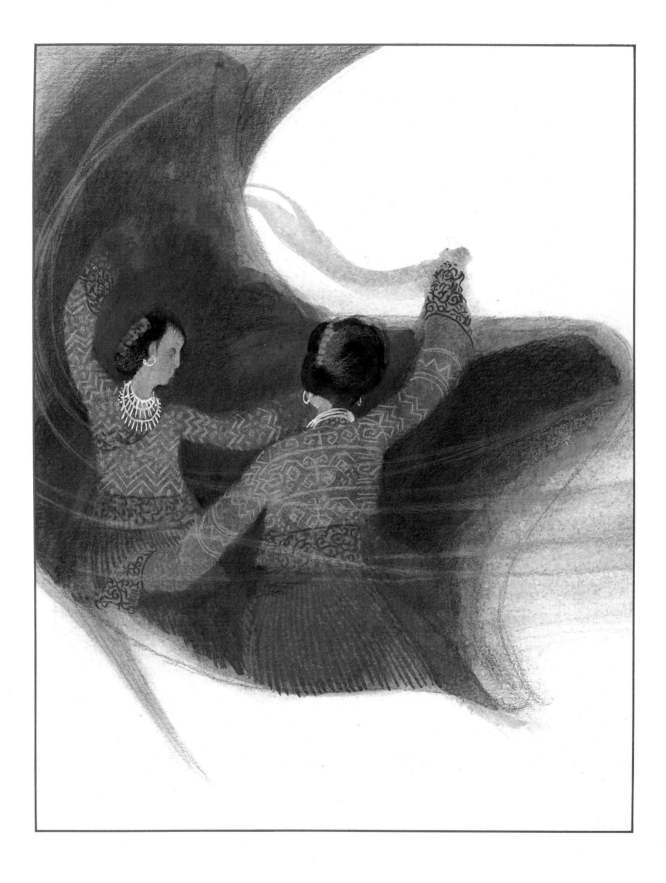

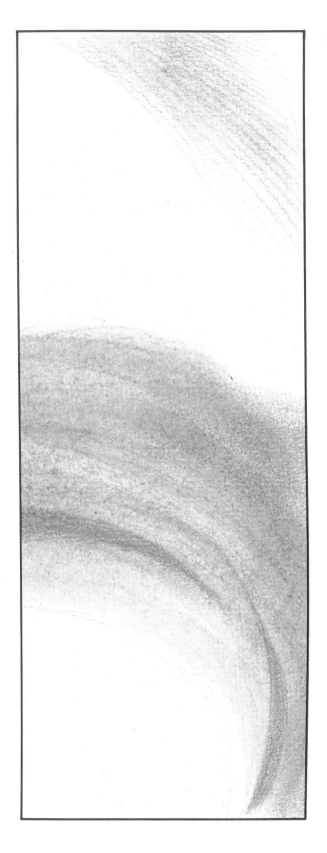

That day Yeh-Shen turned many a head as she appeared at the feast. All around her people whispered, "Look at that beautiful girl! Who can she be?"

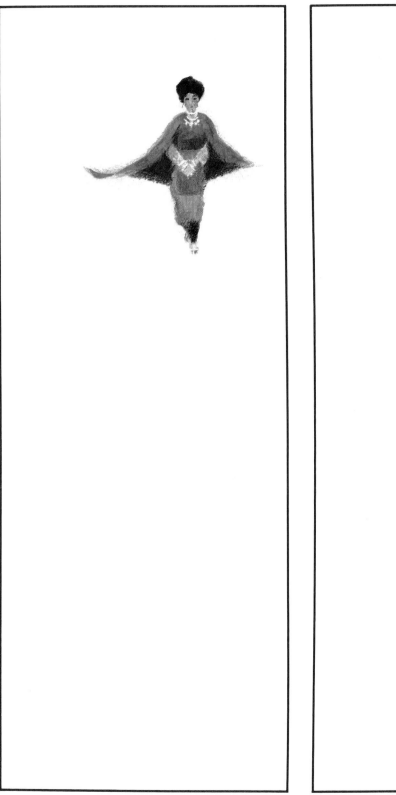

But above this, Stepsister was heard to say, "Mother, does she not resemble our Yeh-Shen?"

Upon hearing this, Yeh-Shen jumped up and ran off before her stepsister could look closely at her. She raced down the mountainside, and in doing so, she lost one of her golden slippers. No sooner had the shoe fallen from her foot than all her fine clothes turned back to rags. Only one thing remained—a tiny golden shoe. Yeh-Shen hurried to the bones of her fish and returned the slipper, promising to find its mate. But now the bones were silent. Sadly Yeh-Shen realized that she had lost her only friend. She hid the little shoe in her bedstraw, and went outside to cry. Leaning against a fruit tree, she sobbed and sobbed until she fell asleep.

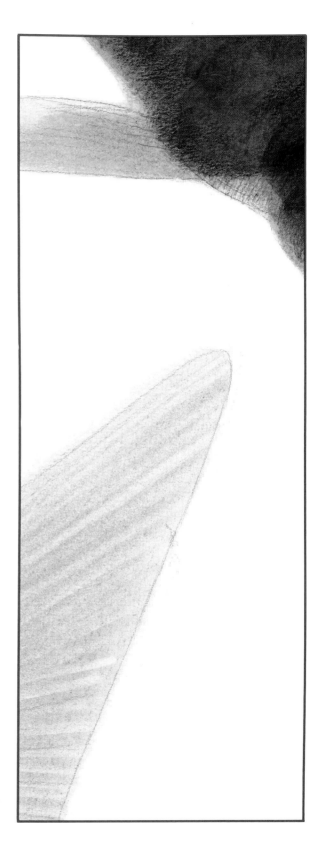

The stepmother left the gathering to check on Yeh-Shen, but when she returned home she found the girl sound asleep, with her arms wrapped around a fruit tree. So thinking no more of her, the stepmother rejoined the party. Meantime, a villager had found the shoe. Recognizing its worth, he sold it to a merchant, who presented it in turn to the king of the island kingdom of T'o Han.

The king was more than happy to accept the slipper as a gift. He was entranced by the tiny thing, which was shaped of the most precious of metals, yet which made no sound when touched to stone. The more he marveled at its beauty, the more determined he became to find the woman to whom the shoe belonged.

A search was begun among the ladies of his own kingdom, but all who tried on the sandal found it impossibly small. Undaunted, the king ordered the search widened to include the cave women from the countryside where the slipper had been found. Since he realized it would take many years for every woman to come to his island and test her foot in the slipper, the king thought of a way to get the right woman to come forward. He ordered the sandal placed in a pavilion by the side of the road near where it

had been found, and his herald announced that the shoe was to be returned to its original owner. Then from a nearby hiding place, the king and his men settled down to watch and wait for a woman with tiny feet to come and claim her slipper.

All that day the pavilion was crowded with cave women who had come to test a foot in the shoe. Yeh-Shen's stepmother and stepsister were among them, but not Yeh-Shen—they had told her to stay home. By day's end, although many women had eagerly tried to put on the slipper, it still had not been worn. Wearily, the king continued his vigil into the night.

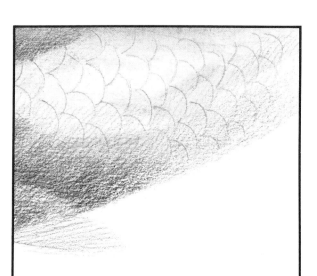

It wasn't until the blackest part of night, while the moon hid behind a cloud, that Yeh-Shen dared to show her face at the pavilion, and even then she tiptoed timidly across the wide floor. Sinking down to her knees, the girl in rags examined the tiny shoe.

Only when she was sure that this was the missing mate to her own golden slipper did she dare pick it up. At last she could return both little shoes to the fish bones. Surely then her beloved spirit would speak to her again.

Now the king's first thought, on

seeing Yeh-Shen take the precious slipper, was to throw the girl into prison as a thief. But when she turned to leave, he caught a glimpse of her face. At once the king was struck by the sweet harmony of her features, which seemed so out of keeping with the rags she wore. It was then that he

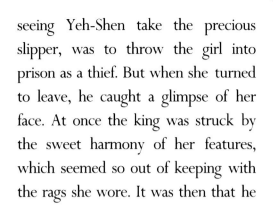

took a closer look and noticed that she walked upon the tiniest feet he had ever seen.

With a wave of his hand, the king signaled that this tattered creature was to be allowed to depart with the golden slipper. Quietly, the king's men slipped off and followed her home.

All this time, Yeh-Shen was unaware of the excitement she had caused. She had made her way home and was about to hide both sandals in her bedding when there was a pounding at the door. Yeh-Shen went to see who it was—and found a king at her doorstep. She was very frightened at first, but the king spoke to her in a kind voice and asked her to try the golden slippers on her feet. The maiden did as she was told, and as she stood in her golden shoes, her rags were transformed once more into the feathered cloak and beautiful azure gown.

Her loveliness made her seem a heavenly being, and the king suddenly knew in his heart that he had found his true love.

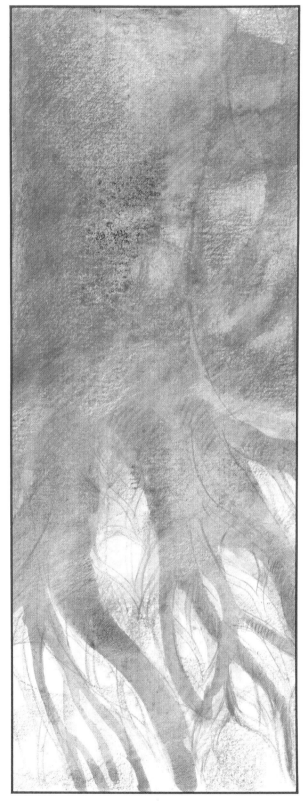

Not long after this, Yeh-Shen was married to the king. But fate was not so gentle with her stepmother and stepsister. Since they had been unkind to his beloved, the king would not permit Yeh-Shen to bring them to his palace. They remained in their cave home, where one day, it is said, they were crushed to death in a shower of flying stones.